HITTY

HER FIRST HUNDRED YEARS

RACHEL FIELD'S

1930 NEWBERY AWARD–WINNING STORY

HITTY

HER FIRST HUNDRED YEARS

A NEW EDITION BY

ROSEMARY WELLS

ILLUSTRATED BY

SUSAN JEFFERS

★

SIMON & SCHUSTER BOOKS FOR YOUNG READERS

For P. J., Jessica, and Melissa —S. J.

★

*The editor and artist wish to thank the wonderful girls and sisters
of the Convent of the Sacred Heart, Greenwich, Connecticut.*

SIMON & SCHUSTER BOOKS FOR YOUNG READERS

An imprint of Simon & Schuster Children's Publishing Division. 1230 Avenue of the
Americas, New York, New York 10020. Text copyright © 1999 by Rosemary Wells.
Illustrations copyright © 1999 by Susan Jeffers. Based on *Hitty: My First Hundred Years* by
Rachel Field/Copyright © 1929 by Macmillan Publishing Company. Copyright renewed
1957 by Arthur S. Pederson. All rights reserved including the right of reproduction in
whole or in part in any form. SIMON & SCHUSTER BOOKS FOR YOUNG READERS is a trademark
of Simon & Schuster. Book design by Susan Jeffers. The text of this book is set in 16-point
Celestia Antiqua. The illustrations are rendered in gouache on cold press watercolor paper.
Printed in the United States of America   1 0 9 8 7 6 5 4 3 2

Library of Congress Cataloging in Publication Data
Wells, Rosemary.
Rachel Field's Hitty, her first hundred years / a new edition by
Rosemary Wells ; illustrated by Susan Jeffers.—1st ed.
p. cm.
Summary: A doll named Hitty recounts her adventures
as she moves through a continually changing
string of owners.
ISBN 0-689-81716-9
[Dolls—Fiction.] I. Field, Rachel, 1894-1942.
Hitty, her first hundred years.
II. Jeffers, Susan, ill.
PZ7.W46843Rac 1999
[Fic]—dc21   97-18683

Note to the Reader

WHEN I WAS young one of the stories I loved best was Rachel Field's *Hitty: Her First Hundred Years*. I read it the way I did all my favorites—at least ten times. I loved Hitty's indomitable spirit and the way time carried her from owner to owner like a river. Hitty didn't mind being stuck in a hayloft for twenty years. Hitty also made American history come alive for me.

As it turned out, *Hitty* was also a favorite of my friend and colleague, Susan Jeffers. Susan wanted to illustrate it with bright, new, colorful pictures. She asked me if I could shorten the story for a new audience.

At first I didn't want to touch it. *Hitty* was one of the best children's books of the whole twentieth century and it had won a Newbery Medal. In my travels, booksellers and librarians told me I was asking for trouble if I adapted a Newbery winner.

But no one I spoke to had actually read *Hitty* in at least thirty years, and that seemed a real shame.

So I decided it was time to dust Hitty off and give her a new lease on life.

What I have done with *Hitty* is much like weeding a beautiful garden. I have cut the length, as I would prune a rose, but the interesting part came as Hitty was about to make her way south just before the Civil War. At this point in the original book Clarissa's sister Ruth almost sends Hitty to a little girl in the South whose doll had been ruined in the war. Almost but not quite. This was my turning point. It was like finding a gold nugget in a rushing stream. I said to myself, "What if Ruth had indeed packed Hitty up and sent her behind Confederate lines?"

You will have to read the book to find out the answer. I will say that when Hitty went south she suddenly belonged to me. Now new live branches flowered and Hitty's adventures tumbled suddenly into a much noisier and more diverse American landscape.

When I was little my grandmother read to me endlessly in her beautiful voice. She was born not long after Rachel Field herself. She spoke the gentle, elegant English of the last century, and held dear the old-fashioned principles of that time and place. I knew if I wrote this story to please my grandmother in my mind's ear, I would get it right. I hope wherever Miss Field is in the cosmos she is pleased with our efforts to give her wonderful Hitty a second hundred years.

Rosemary Wells

CHAPTER ONE
I Begin My Memoirs

THE FIRST WORDS I ever heard were Phoebe Preble's. "Look, Mamma! She's got a real face now!"

The first sight I ever saw was Phoebe's smiling face. She was almost eight years old, and I had been measured and made especially for her.

The peddler who had carved me held me between his thumb and forefinger, turning me around in the firelight so my paint would dry. I was just the right size, with arms and legs that moved on pegs and hair painted hazelnut brown. My first night in the world I was left on the mantelpiece. Shadows from the embers danced on the walls. Mice scampered up and down the wainscoting, and pine branches tapped on the windowpanes.

It was the dead of winter, 1829. The Irish peddler had carved me out of a small piece of mountain ash. It was a treasured piece, and he had brought it across the sea from Kilkenny, Ireland, to the state of Maine. Mountain-ash wood is a good thing to keep close at hand because it brings luck and has power against mischief.

The peddler did business from May to November. Those months were warm enough for farmers' wives and daughters to stand on their doorsteps as he spread out his wares for them to buy. During the winter of '29 he tramped farther north than he had ever been. The gale-force winds heaped drifts of snow across the roads. So he came knocking at the kitchen door of the Preble house, where he had seen a light. He stayed for many snowy weeks, which was a good thing since Phoebe's father, Captain Preble, was away on a ship. In those days, with horses and cows to be tended, huge mounds of snow to be cleared, and ice to be melted for water, one needed a man around the house. Once he was settled, the peddler decided Phoebe needed a doll for her birthday.

Phoebe's mother made me a dress of calico from a left-over quilting square. She wanted me called Mehitabel, but Phoebe was too impatient to use such a long name and I became Hitty instead. Taking out her needle and thread, Phoebe's mother worked these five letters into a cross-stitch on a linen camisole shirt.

"There," said Phoebe's mother. "Now whatever happens to her she can always be sure of her name."

"But nothing is ever going to happen to her, Mother," cried Phoebe, "because she will always be my doll!"

How strange to remember those words now! How little we knew of all that was so soon to happen.

★ ★ ★

When the snow melted and the roads were passable again, the peddler set off. We would have felt lonely without him if Phoebe's father had not turned up shortly after. Captain Preble appeared with treasures from every port he had visited all over the world. There were silk and Paisley scarves, carved ivory elephants, stuffed lizards, and enough knickknacks to fill three shelves of the whatnot.

Phoebe's father kissed her and swung her up over his head two or three times to see how big she had grown.

"This is my new doll, Hitty, Pa!" shouted Phoebe.

Captain Preble was a big man, six feet four in his socks. He had eyes as blue as the spring sky, and the buttons on his coat heaved up and down like little ships at sea when he laughed. "Hitty, is it?" he said. He placed me on his knee as he ate the chowder Mrs. Preble had prepared him and listened to Phoebe tell about the peddler, the piece of mountain ash from Ireland, and the long, cold winter in the middle of Maine.

Phoebe's father had missed her birthday that year, but his present made up for it. It was a matching necklace and bracelet of coral beads from the island of Ceylon. Both strands had a small ivory elephant's head in the middle space. The elephant's eyes were tiny pinpoint gold dots. Phoebe asked her father to shorten the bracelet into a necklace for me, and he did. He restrung the beads and elephant head on silver-thread fish line and tied it in a fisherman's knot.

"It will never break or come undone," Captain Preble told Phoebe. And he was right. Over the next hundred years of my adventures, my elephant-head necklace never left my throat, and it later turned out to be the key to my rediscovery. ✦

4

CHAPTER TWO
I Travel—by Land and Sea

 UMMER IN NORTHERN Maine feels as if it is trying to make up all at once for the long darkness of winter. The sunny sky looks almost worried, it is so very blue and the clouds are so perfectly powder-white. Phoebe said she could hear the garden unfolding and growing all night long if she went to her window and listened.

Captain Preble took Phoebe and me out in a small pumpkin-colored dory and taught her to sail in a pond. In August Phoebe had learned enough to take the boat out by herself, and from it we could reach berry patches almost no one else knew existed.

The best patch was sheltered by a stand of junipers. I was always placed on a

mossed-over stump, easy to find and away from harm. When the wind blew from the west the air smelled sharp and piney. When it blew from the east it smelled salty and fishy.

Only Penobscot women knew about this berry patch and picked there. Phoebe and I went out every morning with an old tin pail and she plucked until her fingers were purple.

"Over this summer, Hitty," Phoebe said to me, "I've learned to sail, learned to roll out a piecrust without breaking it, and I've learned the Penobscot words for huckleberry and blackberry. What do you think?"

I thought, What more could anyone want to learn?

★ ✦ ★

Captain Preble rode to Portland three times every week to see if the mail had brought him news of his ship the *Diana-Kate*. There was never any news, and by September the captain grew impatient.

"Guess I'll have to go down to Boston if we expect to weigh anchor and ship out before November," he told his wife one day.

"Now, Daniel, don't you go off before I get your twelfth pair of socks knitted," his wife begged. "I couldn't rest easy here at home if I thought you was sloshing around in wet feet!"

"Come along to Boston with me tomorrow," he suggested. "You can finish the socks on the way and fit yourself and Phoebe out with new winter woolens in style."

It was a warm September morning when we all set off to catch the Boston stage. I sat in Phoebe's lap and watched the miles go by as the carriage rocked and jumped over the muddy Post Road. The bright yellow of elm leaves and the flaming red of woodbine made the fences look as if they had burst into flame.

"There, Kate," said the captain, suddenly pointing with his whip, "that's the first mountain ash I've seen this fall."

"That's Hitty's tree," cried Phoebe, "and it's magic!"

"Hush, child," reproved her mother, "you mustn't say such things."

"But the Irish peddler said so, Mother," Phoebe insisted. "Don't you remember when he was making her he said it was a charm against evil?"

"Well, now, I guess he was just giving you a fish story," put in the captain. "Anyhow, it's a pretty sight."

★ ★ ★

By the next evening we were settled in Boston, in a couple of rooms that an elderly lady rented out to sailors' families. From the upper windows of her house

Boston harbor looked like a bouncing forest of ship masts.

Phoebe and I were in bed by the time Captain Preble returned from his ship, the *Diana-Kate*. Some of his best men were sick, and he could not find a proper cook. This seemed to worry him most of all. Ships' cooks were hard to find.

That night he had a long talk with Phoebe's mother. I could not hear much of what they said, since Phoebe and I were in bed and they talked with their heads close together. Captain Preble spread charts out before him, and his wife

listened to him as he pointed things out to her with his big forefinger.

"Well, Daniel," she said when he was through, "I'll take the night to think it over and let you know by morning. I never counted on going to sea, least of all to cook for a parcel of hungry men in one of those greasy old 'blubber-hunters' as you call 'em."

But by breakfast time the next morning it was all settled that we should go.

We got down to the wharves after sunset, but I could still make out the dark outlines of hulls and moving men in the light of the autumn evening.

"There she is," said the captain suddenly, pointing to a looming shape alongside of the wharf. "That's your new home, Phoebe. Reckon you're goin' to like it?"

Captain Preble did not ask me, but if I could have, I would have answered with a hearty yes.

We were swung aboard like so many packages. High overhead the masthead lantern gleamed whitely in a circle of paler light it sent out into the darkness.

And so our voyage began. ✦

CHAPTER THREE

We Go to Sea

 AIM TO PUT out by four o'clock," I heard Captain Preble say to Andy, the cabin boy, "and we'll make the tide serve us out."

I thought it was very nice of the tide to be willing to serve us. It is amazing how ignorant I was then of the simplest sea phrases.

All the first night aboard Phoebe and I slid and slipped on a cracked leather sofa. Overhead were rattlings and squeakings, grinding of chains, and clumping of boots on the wooden decks.

When Phoebe carried me up on deck the next morning, we found the *Diana-Kate* running before the wind. Her square sails billowed out, and her bow lifted

over great blue-green waves, the like
of which I had never imagined.

Phoebe was soon measured for the new
bunk and I for a rope hammock that the sailor
named Elijah had promised to make. The strong sea
sunshine felt so good, with the big sails throwing shadows on
each other, that I felt only pleasure as I looked out on the tossing blue water before us.

Phoebe was only a little seasick those first days out, the rest of us not a bit. Mrs. Preble made a batch of molasses cookies big enough for all, a rare treat indeed for a whaling ship in those days.

I was proud when Elijah said, after Phoebe told him about my being made of mountain ash, that he had no doubt I would bring them good luck.

"She ought to be as much good to us as old lady Diana Kate down yonder," he said, pointing toward the ship's figurehead. Attached to the prow of the ship just under the bowsprit, she was a beautiful wood carving of the top half of a woman.

Poor Diana Kate. Up and down she pitched, drenched in salt spray whenever the ship took any big wave. I, on the other hand, enjoyed privileges, especially the hammock Elijah had made me. All the sailors were clever at making things from odds and ends. Before long I had a basket, a carved bone footstool, and a sea chest to hold all my possessions. The chest was the gift of Seaman Bill Buckle. It was painted bright red, with rope handles and my initials, H. P., picked out in shiny nail heads on the lid.

Bill Buckle and Andy, the cabin boy, were our best friends. Bill showed us his tattoos. There were mermaids in green on one arm, sea serpents in red on the other, while a clipper ship in full rig and three colors sailed straight across his back.

★ ★ ★

One night I heard Captain Preble tell his wife the only thing that bothered him was that "everything was going too well." Just when that was I can't remember. Soon after, we reached the mysterious place called Cape Horn, and the *Diana-Kate* struck bad weather. The storm hit suddenly late one afternoon. We only just had time to lash the sails and batten the hatches before we were in the teeth of it.

"Now don't you get worried, Kate," Captain Preble told his wife. He took a last look

around the cabin to make sure all was tight before going on deck. "It won't be exactly smooth sailing for a spell, but I've put through worse'n this is goin' to be."

"Well, put on an extra pair of socks, Daniel, and take your muffler aloft," was all she said, but I could see that she was scared to death. Long before bedtime, she tied Phoebe and me to her bunk with an old piece of flannel.

"Can't have you falling down and breaking your bones," her mother warned when Phoebe complained. "We've got trouble enough as it is."

Only a dim and smoky oil lamp hung in the main cabin just outside. The ship plunged and swung crazily, making eerie shadows that frightened Phoebe into tears. She finally ducked her head under the blankets and held me close against her.

We were no better off in the morning. Water poured down whenever the hatchway was opened and leaked in every time a wave broke over the *Diana-Kate*'s bow and washed her decks with tons of saltwater.

"You'd best stay in your bunk same as Phoebe," the Captain told Mrs. Preble on one of his few trips below. "I'd send one of the crew down to help you, but truth is I

can't spare a one of 'em. She's sprung a leak and it takes four men to bail her out."

"Mercy, Daniel!" I heard Mrs. Preble cry out. "Ain't that pretty bad?"

"Well, I can't say it's exactly good," he answered as he stood by the cabin door gulping down some hot tea she had brought him in a tin cup. "Trouble is we can't patch the hole till the storm lets up. But it's bound to if we can just ride it out."

The wind howled and tore at the masts till I thought they would crack in two. We could feel the *Diana-Kate* shiver, and then came a sound of such horrid ripping and splintering that it terrifies me now to think of it. Captain Preble bellowed out

commands in a voice that sounded no bigger than a cricket.

"Cut her away, boys!" he was shouting. "Let her go—topsail and all!"

"What's happened? Are we going to sink?" Phoebe cried, seeing the fright in her mother's face.

"Not if your father can help it," her mother answered, but her eyes were enormous. She was standing in water to her ankles.

After that the captain came back and told us the main mast had been cut away from the ship and had gone over the side. "And we are lucky we didn't follow it!" he added.

"Oh, but it's Hitty who's saved us," said Phoebe, sitting up and getting out of the bunk at last. "She's made of mountain ash and she's very lucky, you know. If it weren't for Hitty we'd all be at the bottom of the sea." ✦

CHAPTER FOUR

We Strike Our First and Last Whale

THE *DIANA-KATE*'S leak was patched and a new topsail and mast concocted. We headed for the whaling grounds of the South Seas. The harpoons were sharpened and the ropes tarred in readiness for the first cry from the lookout that he saw a whale coming up to blow.

As the days grew hotter Phoebe Preble shed her merino dress, then her knitted stockings, then her flannel petticoats, and last of all her curls. These were sheared off by Elijah. When he had finished, Phoebe's mother almost cried.

"This is what comes of taking her to sea," she lamented. "You wouldn't know her for the same child we took aboard."

Her father could not deny this. In those days little girls were not supposed to be suntanned and freckled. But he only laughed at his wife's head-shakings.

"Guess I'll get Jim to cut down those old trousers of Andy's. We won't be in a port for months, so who cares how she looks?" he said.

Phoebe and Andy and I saw the first whale from the deck. A faraway jet of water spouted like a fountain. Five boats at once went out for the chase. The men rowed with all their might.

"Greasy luck, boys!" called Captain Preble as he watched them go.

How should I, a little wooden doll, be able to tell of such things—of those boats that looked no bigger than pea pods, scurrying through the water toward that enormous gray shape that appeared and disappeared so mysteriously. I cannot believe that I did actually see this for myself.

Andy pressed close to the low rail, shading his eyes with his hands.

"There it is!" he cried, so shrilly Phoebe almost dropped me over the side. "See it spout! Elijah's boat's ahead. I can tell by his red and white shirt."

The little slip of a boat seemed about to vanish under the glistening mass of whale towering over it. Then Elijah struck with his harpoon. The whale dragged the boat after him as he plunged under the water, trying to escape. Finally the mountainous body rose a little more out of the water, then turned over slowly until a black fin stood straight up.

The whale was stretched out at full

length along the side of the ship and tied with ropes and pulleys. The men peeled off the blubber in long strips as neatly as if they were paring skin from an apple. Then it was chopped into smaller pieces and put into the try-pots, where it was boiled into oil over fires that burned night and day. I wondered how there would be any whale oil left, so much of it ran over the decks. But no one paid any attention to this except Mrs. Preble, who said she had never in all her days smelled such a smell or seen such a mess of grease. The men only laughed. They would each be paid well for their share of whale oil, which everyone back home used to light their lamps. Though the killing of the whales seems cruel and heartless, at the time it was necessary.

Thick smoke hung over us like an umbrella. The men worked with only a few hours off for rest.

"Got to push so we can go after another," Captain Preble explained as he came to eat his supper, hands so stiff from the work of cutting-in that he could scarcely hold his knife and fork.

It must have been around midnight when I heard the thudding of feet hammering above us. Then the call: "All hands on deck!"

Phoebe woke and wanted to go above, but her mother said she would only get in the men's way. So we three waited in the darkness.

Suddenly Captain Preble was at the door, his eyes red and watering. "The ship's afire," he told us quietly.

Mrs. Preble clung to him suddenly as if she were no bigger than Phoebe. "Oh, Daniel, what chance have we got?"

"Better get some things together," he cautioned her, "in case . . ." His face showed pale under the smudges of ash, but he squared his shoulders and went above.

Phoebe packed my things—the red chest, the footstool, and my hammock. Then she dressed me and laid me beside them in a basket.

"Come along, Phoebe," said her mother. "If there's any trouble I don't aim to stay cooped up down here."

Starlight reflected on the still water. Most of the crew had jumped ship. The *Diana-Kate* hardly stirred. We could not see the flames because the wet canvases were still down, but rolls of eye-watering, choking smoke curled up from between the boards.

A rope ladder had been let down to the lifeboats.

"Mercy!" cried Phoebe's mother. "I'll never be able to go down that."

"You hold on to me, ma'am," Elijah told her. "Hoist your petticoats and don't stand on no ceremony."

So over the side she went, hand over hand, with Elijah going first in case she should let go.

Andy and Bill Buckle came up with some kegs of food and water. Captain Preble had his small compass, a lantern, and the log book. A smear of soot ran like a scar across one cheek. His eyes were swollen.

Phoebe set me down in the basket on top of a large water keg. Suddenly her father scooped her up in his arms and hustled her over the side and into the boat. This all happened in the twinkling of an eye. I thought I heard Phoebe calling from below, but the others were making too much noise for me to hear her. I knew she must be asking for me, and this did not make me feel any easier.

The next minute I expected my turn to come—but it never did.

Just as it seemed the paint on my face would sizzle, the ship gave a lurch. Out I tumbled and into the water as neatly as a pebble from a sling shot. ★

CHAPTER FIVE

I Join the Fishes and Rejoin the Prebles

ALL ALONE, I floated in miles of salty sea and tropical sun. Burned bits of the *Diana-Kate* bobbed alongside of me. Fishes with rainbow scales and blue lips nibbled at me. Elijah had talked of sailors joining the fishes, which meant drowning, but of course they were not made of mountain ash. I was sure that sooner or later a shark or a whale would gulp me down with a mouthful of seawater, but they didn't seem to like the cut of my jib, and once again Lady Luck watched over me.

Within a day and night I found myself drifting in the quiet of a rock pool. Seaweeds trailed scarlet tendrils in its clear water. I wanted only to lie still in the shade after all the batterings I had suffered.

And then I heard voices close by. I knew them. They were Andy and Bill Buckle. Oh, I thought, to be able to cry out to them just once!

Fortunately, Andy saw me. He grabbed me, shook the water from me, and carried me back in triumph.

"I declare if it ain't a miracle!" Mrs. Preble exclaimed as Phoebe held me close to her heart. "Wherever did you find her, Andy?"

"Down in one of those crab pools," he explained with pride.

"Well, it certainly beats all," Captain Preble remarked, smiling at my face. "It takes us the better part of a day to row here, charts and rudder and four pair of oars, and she gets here all by herself with no trouble at all."

"I always said that doll would bring us luck," put in Elijah, "and I say so now. I don't care who hears me."

There was no one besides us to hear him except some brightly colored birds and a number of small brown animals with long tails. These,

I learned, were called "monkeys," and I was to see more of them in the days to come.

Phoebe repaired my clothes then and there. They dried fast in the glaring sunlight, and soon I was presentable once more, though tattered and faded.

Palm trees grew on the island. Ferns and pink hibiscus flowers filled the jungle. Trees hung thick with fruits and the coconuts that the monkeys were forever after. Mrs. Preble did not think much of the coconuts, but Phoebe and Andy loved them after the long diet of ship's biscuits and salt meat.

We spent our first night on the island in a grass hut. The darkness was warm and filled with strange noises from outside. The bright stars cheered Captain Preble, but Mrs. Preble said they were all in the wrong places from where she was used to seeing them and it only made her feel farther from home.

Every day the captain looked through his spyglass to see if there were signs of other ships on the horizon. Our longboat was kept ready to launch at the first topsail that should appear. One morning he reported smoke coming from a distant hillside. Then Elijah raced up from shore to say that a navy of outrigger canoes was heading our way. Phoebe and I sat in the door of the hut and listened to the talk that went on. It reminded me of the moments before a thunderstorm.

No one knew whether the islanders would be friendly or not, but it was best to be prepared for anything.

"You're to do whatever I tell you," her father told Phoebe, "no matter what it is. Do you understand?"

"Yes, Father," she answered.

Andy had very sharp eyes, and after some time he could make out that there were many boats, all keeping close together as they approached.

"They're heading this way sure enough," he said.

A band of men edged up from shore. Some carried spears, others had painted shields. Captain Preble beckoned us to come and stand beside him. Mrs. Preble took Phoebe's hand and we followed him out into the sunshine. Dozens of bright-eyed strangers peered at us.

Bill Buckle took off his shirt and showed off his tattoos. This caused a murmur to go from mouth to mouth. They crowded around him until I thought he would be crushed by all the pressing bodies.

Then Phoebe caught their attention. She had kept me hidden behind her back, but the biggest islander, with the most rings and beads, caught sight of me. Phoebe clutched me tight against her. The islander made a signal to the rest. I could feel Phoebe's heart thump, but she stood firm even when the big man touched me with one enormous finger. Then he held out his hand to her.

I heard the captain's voice say, "Give her to him, Phoebe."

"Not Hitty, Father—" I heard Phoebe falter.

"You give her to him and you do it quick." Only on the day of the fire on the *Diana-Kate* had I ever before heard the captain speak that way.

The next thing I knew I was staring into the chief's lively black eyes. He held me respectfully and called his brothers to his side. Phoebe reached out for me, but Bill Buckle quickly pulled her hand back.

"Steady," he cautioned. "Don't you make no sign of wanting her." Then he added, "They've got spears and there's more of them than of us."

The chief lifted me up for all to see before they took me back to their canoes. Well, Hitty, said I to myself, queer things have happened to you—in the state of Maine and out of it—but this is certainly the queerest! ✦

CHAPTER SIX
I Learn the Ways of Gods and Monkeys

HE ISLANDER CHIEF gave me to a young boy I assumed was his son. The boy set me on an altar trimmed with hibiscus flowers in a tiny temple of leaves and bamboo shoots. As soon as the flowers drooped, he brought fresh ones, and also small offerings in the way of fruits and shells.

He smeared purple berry juice in designs on my face and body. I liked better the flowers and a lump of red coral he hung around my neck. He invited all of his friends to come and look at me, but I could not understand a word of the islander language. It is lonely to be a god for days on end.

During this time I came to know monkeys and their ways. There was a smallish one with a silvery-white face and whippy little tail who loved to hang and make faces at me from a banyan tree.

One day he came closer than he ever had before. I felt his breath on my face. Then his hand reached into the temple and closed around me as if I were a banana. Whisked off my altar, I sped in his hand through the trees until suddenly he stopped, panicky. I heard the English language for the first time in many a long week.

It was Andy who had spotted us both. He began hurling clamshells thick and fast. One of them clipped my monkey friend on the ear, and he dropped me and skittled off.

"Hitty! What are you doing here?" Andy asked. Straight to the beach he ran with me. I had no idea why Andy was in such a hurry until I saw the Prebles and everyone else gathered there. I could tell in a minute that another ship had been sighted and we were to set out and signal her.

I could just make out the dark shapes of Captain Preble and the rest in the evening light. Phoebe and her mother were already in the stern seat of the boat.

"Where on earth have you been, Andy?" the captain scolded.

Andy drew me out from behind his back.

"I found Hitty," he explained, holding me out. At this Phoebe started to stand up in the boat, so that it rocked furiously.

"Sit down, Phoebe!" commanded her father. "Yes, it's Hitty, right enough."

"It won't be no tea party if his Nibs, the chief, finds she's gone and the troops decide to come after us!" warned Bill Buckle.

Phoebe held me so close to her that a tidal wave could not have ripped me away. "Oh, Mother," she sighed, "when we get home I'll give Andy my silver mug to keep forever."

"Never mind that," said Mrs. Preble. "The ship we sighted has gone over the horizon. If we don't find her again and if she don't see our lantern we daren't go back to the island. Pray, child, pray!"

"We ought to sight her any minute now," the captain kept telling them. But as the minutes turned into hours and still no masthead lantern loomed ahead, the men grew silent, pulling hard and wasting no breath on words or questions.

Suddenly Andy gave a cry. "There it is!" he shouted. "On our port side, plain as anything!"

Captain Preble lit our signal lantern with an excited hand.

An hour passed and then another with no sign of the ship spotting our light. The men rowed toward it and the captain burned the last of the lamp oil for our signal. Our wick gave out and Captain Preble burned his only coat, then Mrs. Preble's favorite woolen shawl.

Then I saw his hands go out in a quick gesture. Another light had appeared beside the other. Now another and another shot up.

"They've sighted us, praise be!" he cried. "They're sendin' up flares to tell us they're coming."

Elijah slumped down in his seat with his face between his hands, and Bill Buckle and Andy were sobbing like Mrs. Preble and Phoebe. I would have cried, too, if I had been able. ★

CHAPTER SEVEN

I Am Lost in India

WE WERE TAKEN aboard the *Hesper* and before long felt as much at home there as on the *Diana-Kate*. Her captain hailed from our part of the world, Massachusetts, where he had left a wife and children. I shall always remember him with gratitude because after seeing the sorry state of my clothes, he offered his best handkerchief to wrap me in. It was of rich blue silk with anchors and twisted ropes woven all round the border.

Phoebe entertained the new crew with stories of my adventures with the islanders and showed them where my purple stains had been.

"D'you think she'll miss being a god when she gets home to Maine?" asked the second mate.

Phoebe said she didn't think so, and neither did I.

We sighted land and pulled into port at Bombay, India. The *Hesper*'s captain wanted to bring his daughter a sari, and he said that Phoebe should have one, too. Captain Preble told his wife to find the handsomest new shawl in the city.

By noon we had collected three embroidered saris. Whatever caught Phoebe Preble's fancy found its way into her hands or her father's pockets. She soon had gold bracelets and strings of mother-of-pearl and cowrie shells.

She stopped everyone in front of another stall. "Hitty must have something, too," said Phoebe. She picked out a silk scarf edged in gold. Phoebe declared I would soon be a queen among dolls. Little did we guess that this was to be our last day together!

We saw elephants led in a procession through the streets. We bargained in bazaars and Phoebe ate curry and sweetmeats. By midafternoon she began to lag. Bill Buckle took her in his arms and soon we were jogging comfortably. I felt happy, as is so often the case when we have the least reason to be.

Her head dropped lower and lower until she was fast asleep. I dangled from Phoebe's hand, which hung over Bill's shoulder. Suddenly I felt myself slipping. I fell free of them both, flat on my face in an unknown gutter.

★ ★ ★

I never saw Phoebe or any of the Preble family again. She must be dead a good many years now, even if she lived to be a very old lady, for that was almost one hundred years ago and she was not made of mountain ash.

My next memory is of being lifted up by swiftly moving fingers. These belonged to a man in a turban. He seemed about to toss me away again, then, wiping me off, he took me with him.

Next thing I knew I was in a dark room, close to a wicker basket. From the basket came the strangest rustlings. I knew that no good whatsoever could come out of that basket. I would have given my coral beads and silk-scarf dress to be out of its way.

Unhappy as I was, I could not help but watch in horrified fascination as the turbaned man crouched nearby and drew a bamboo flute from under his robes. The basket twitched. The cover quivered and rose inch by inch from within, then *pop!* The top flipped and the head and body of a great hooded cobra swerved out. It uncoiled and slipped from the basket, creeping toward the flute player. He stopped his music and the snake also stopped in the midst of a glide. Then he played more quickly and the cobra grew more excited. The bright, lidless eyes glittered and the forked tongue darted. Once, part of its chilly body slid across my feet. Had my hair not been painted on my head it would have stood on end.

Still, as I have said, one can get used to anything in time— even great hooded cobras. After several days I learned to take him more calmly.

I lost all track of time. We must have traveled all the latitudes and longitudes of India. My only role was to stand by while the flute player and his snake went through their performance. I was sure I would end my days in heat and dust, far from my native state of Maine. Which only goes to show how little any of us can tell about what is in store for us.

One evening the snake charmer set down his basket in front of a circle of children. Out came the flute and snake. As usual, I had been set beside the basket, still wrapped in the now tattered blue handkerchief. Just as the cobra was sliding toward its master I heard a voice saying words that I could understand. They were very simple words, but I can't tell you how much homesickness and relief they brought to me in that place.

"Hurry, my dear," was what I heard. "We'll be late getting home."

A man and woman stood far back watching the snake charmer perform. Their plain clothes were like those at home. Something must have caught the woman's eye for she plucked at the man's sleeve. Then she pointed toward me.

There I was, unable to move so much as a single peg to express my joy, or to beg them to rescue me. But luck or the power of mountain ash intervened. The lady said, "Look at her face and hair, William. She couldn't have been made anywhere but home."

He agreed. "She reminds me of my sister Ruth back in Delaware. What would you think of buying her for Thankful?" he said. "Here she is growing up so far from home and not even a doll to play with."

"She looks a little dirty," said the lady.

"Well, we ought to be able to fix that," he answered with a smile. "Think of all the souls we came here to wash clean of their sins."

The man could speak the Hindu language, and he bargained for me. His wife took my tattered handkerchief dress off immediately as if it might be full of bugs. "Hitty," she said, reading my camisole. "Well, Hitty it is."

I was happy to get a scrubbing with soap and water. During my bath I learned I had fallen into the hands of missionaries. In the middle of India they nursed and converted as many native Indians as possible to the Presbyterian religion. Their only child, Thankful, was about to get me for her sixth birthday. ★

CHAPTER EIGHT

I Have Another Child to Play with Me

THANKFUL'S MOTHER WAS better at Bible lessons than at dressing dolls. She made me a large dress of plain cotton print. It nearly covered my feet, and the collar hid my coral necklace. But I was clean and comfortable and I belonged to a little girl again. It was high time she had a doll, and though Thankful never lavished the same amount of care and affection on me as Phoebe Preble did, she never treated me unkindly, until—but I have not reached that yet.

Mission life was very quiet up in the remote hills of India. We slept under mosquito netting in the heat of the nights. The midday sun stopped everyone in their tracks, and as we sat indoors, Thankful's mother taught her to read and write and count up to fifty. She also taught her hymns.

One day Thankful fell ill with a serious fever. Her father and mother used one after another of their best remedies, but nothing worked. When the fever edged up to 104 degrees, Thankful's Indian nurse slipped into the sickroom with a native doctor. Thoughtfully he studied the little girl in the big bed, felt her hands and forehead. Then he prescribed herbs and directions for brewing them. The nurse knew that Thankful's parents would not approve of native treatment, so she did this all in secret, but it worked. Thankful recovered.

I overheard Thankful's father say, "This is no climate for children."

Her mother answered, "It will break my heart not to see her again for five years, but it would be best for her to go back to Mother in Philadelphia."

"Yes," he said. "We will miss her terribly but she must go home."

Go we did. Friends of another mission offered to care for Thankful on the long voyage.

Once again I found myself a passenger aboard a sailing ship, this time homeward bound. After a week at sea, Thankful's parents would scarcely have known her. She ran all over the ship as Phoebe Preble had done, though she was not as brave at climbing the ratlines. Her sandy hair, usually kept brushed as smooth as satin, now blew wildly about. Her face became a swath of freckles to the square inch, and the ruffles of her petticoats were in tatters. If the good ladies sent to care for her from the Presbyterian mission tried to do anything about this, Thankful raced out of their sight with the swiftness of a squirrel.

From my porthole I could see water and hear the chanteys the men sang as they hauled on their lines. Every day brought me nearer home. The ship passed the shores of the Carolinas, and after that it was only a few days before we docked.

We drove through Philadelphia's brick-lined streets very early one morning as Thankful's grandfather took us to his house. It was a sunny April day, and the hooves of the matched pair of horses clattered over the cobblestones. Someone was out scouring steps or polishing brass door knockers everywhere I looked. I felt happier than I had since I became parted from the Prebles.

Thankful's grandmother's hair was as white as Maine snow. At the end of her sleeves were the most dimpled pair of hands I have ever seen. She bustled and rustled a great deal that first day, making little clicking noises with her teeth over the sorry state of her granddaughter's clothes.

"Dear, dear," she sighed to her husband, "it's worse than I expected. The poor child hasn't even a merino or a dimity to her name, and as for her bodices and her undermuslins, it really pains me to think that a grandchild of mine should be in this condition. It will take time to outfit her properly, and I promised the Pryces she should go to Janet Pryce's party tomorrow."

Thankful was excited at the idea, for it was to be her first party, and mine. Her grandmother took us out shopping in the morning. I was dazzled by all the fine stores. In those days ready-made dresses had not been invented. Instead, material was bought by the yard and nimble-fingered dressmakers stayed at a house for weeks in order to fit out different members of the family.

Morocco leather slippers were purchased. When a peach-colored sash was draped around Thankful, and when her hair was brushed smooth and a blue enamel locket added, her grandmother said she would do. She didn't know how they would ever get rid of all those dreadful freckles and threatened to use lemon juice to bleach them out. Thankful found a silk hanky, which she wrapped about me, and she pulled my necklace out to show as much as possible.

The Pryces' house was only a few doors distant. Janet's mother, also in swishing silk, greeted us and kissed Thankful warmly. We were taken to a parlor completely filled with little girls. With their bright dresses and glistening curls, they looked like a flock of tropical butterflies. I had no idea that they were not as sweet as their appearance. No sooner were the grown-up people out of the way than the girls started giggling and whispering things to each other about Thankful's appearance.

"If that's the way they dress in India, I'll certainly never go there," said one young miss in flowered dimity.

"What makes you have so many freckles?" asked another, peering at Thankful very rudely, "and why don't you wear curls and ruffles all the way up your skirts?"

The things they said about me! I was "an ugly old thing," and I looked as if the cat had fished me out of the dump heap. Thankful stared back at these beautiful birthday party girls as if they were strange animals with dreadful claws. My expression remained pleasant as always, but my temper burned at these insults.

The guests set their own dolls on the sofa. These were big dolls with beautifully glazed china heads with real hair and glass eyes. Their dresses were silk and satin and lace. I was the only one who was wooden and as simply dressed as a farm girl.

When everyone crowded around Janet's birthday cake, Thankful slipped away. She ran over to the dolls' sofa. I thought she was coming to get me so I could share in the party. But, no! She grabbed me and stuffed me into the crevice where the arm and seat of the sofa fitted together. Her fingers pushed me deep out of sight. Had I been made of anything but stout ash wood, I feel sure I should have snapped in two, but somehow or other I survived.

I lay in the dark sofa innards, cramped and rejected. Thankful ran back to the other room. It was not possible, I thought, that she could have deserted me. But Thankful did not come back. ★

CHAPTER NINE
I Am Rescued and Join the Quakers

 OON AFTER THE birthday party, the sofa was sent up to the attic. I felt it hoisted on the shoulders of two men, who carried it up several flights of stairs. After that there was nothing to see or hear. Moths and an occasional nibbling mouse were my only visitors for fifteen years. I could not reason out what on earth I had ever done to deserve such terrible rejection. Human beings, I decided, were not nearly as faithful as dolls.

Then, finally, on a rainy afternoon a passel of children visited the attic.

"Let's play train!" one suggested.

I had no idea what trains were, though I learned about them soon enough.

Those children did their best to be as noisy as the loudest steam engine. They bounced up and down above me and beat their feet against the framework till I expected us all to collapse together. Just as I wished the sofa would fall apart, I felt a hand poke in. Imagine my joy when it actually closed around my waist!

The next thing I knew faces were peering over me, and they were poking and hooting with curiosity.

"It's a doll!" they cried. "How ever do you suppose it got into that old sofa?"

I was adopted by Clarissa Pryce. She was a niece of the Janet Pryce who had hosted the birthday party. Janet was now grown-up with children of her own and lived in Kansas City.

Clarissa celebrated her tenth birthday soon after I was found. She was delicate, with gray eyes and the softest red hair. Her hands were gentle, and she was more skillful with needle and thread than Phoebe or Thankful. The day she found me she began to make me a dress. Immediately she found my name. "Thee must have been thought of highly, Hitty," she said, "to wear a coral necklace and thy name in cross-stitch, too."

I was a little puzzled by her talk until I learned that the Pryces were Quakers, who always call each other "thee" instead of "you." This meant that I was no longer an outsider but a real member of the Pryce family. Each of my two outfits could be taken on and off. One of these was brown calico to be worn six days of the week, and the other was a pearl-gray silk, made in true Quaker fashion for First Day, as the Pryces called Sunday.

Clarissa's older sister, Ruth, made me a desk with a lid from a soap box. Clarissa cut me sheets of paper the size of a postage stamp. She gave me a quill pen from a feather shed by a neighbor's parrot. The Quakers wore only plain colors, and the feather was such a shocking bright yellow and scarlet that I was afraid Mrs. Pryce would say it was much too gaudy for a Quaker doll. But she did not object, because the parrot had been given these colors by nature. So I spent many happy days at my writing desk.

★ ★ ★

One cold day in February in the year 1861 we had a visitor. He was a German boy named Paul Schneider who delivered sausages from his father's pushcart.

"Such a huzzle buzzle is happening this afternoon!" Paul said to Clarissa. "Mr. Abraham Lincoln, the new president, is coming through Philadelphia. He will give a speech at Rittenhouse Square. I am going to see him."

"Oh lucky you," said Clarissa.

Paul smiled. "My pappa plays the french horn in the City Marching Band," he said. "He has special seats right next to the stage. You come, too!"

Clarissa hushed Paul. "Mamma and Pappa are going out to the opera matinee this afternoon. They always want me to stay home safe from crowds and pickpockets."

Paul whispered, "I will stop back at two and see if you change your mind."

All morning Clarissa went round in circles. I heard it all. "If I ask them, they'll say no," she reasoned. "If I don't ask, then I won't be disobeying or breaking my word. But of course that would be dishonesty of the heart."

It was Paul's father who decided for Clarissa. He came with Paul to the kitchen door.

"Your mamma and pappa have left for the opera?" he asked.

"Yes," said Clarissa.

"Then there is no one to ask," he reasoned. "I will bring you home safe and sound!"

We four went bounding down the street toward Rittenhouse Square. All was well until we came to the corner of Franklin and Main. There the crowds swarmed

so thickly they reminded me of my days in India. Paul's father drew us to the shelter of a doorway.

"Wait here until they pass," he said. "They are on their way to the opera house to hear the great soprano Adalina Patti sing. Soon the streets will be clear again."

Mr. Schneider knew his onions. People flocked to the opera house like a thousand moths flying to a single candle. A much smaller crowd braved the cold toward the folding seats set out in a semicircle in front of a flag-draped stage.

Suddenly a Rockingham wagon clattered to a halt beside us. It nearly tipped over from a fallen-off wheel. A gentleman in a black suit unfolded his gangly body and

opened the door of the carriage. His face looked as if it had been carved in stone and not quite finished. He took off his jacket and looked at the damage under the wagon.

"Are you, by any chance, Mr. President Lincoln?" asked Clarissa shyly.

The gentleman kneeled in the gutter just at eye level with Clarissa, examining the axle where the wheel had come away. "I am," he answered with an unhappy sigh. "And a power of good it does me. If I were back in Illinois I'd have this fixed in no time. But they don't give spare pins and mallets to the president of the United States!"

Mr. Lincoln took Clarissa's hand to shake it. She was so surprised she dropped me right on the sidewalk. "That's no way to treat a lady!" Mr. Lincoln told her with a chuckle, rescuing me in the biggest right hand that had ever held me before or since. His teeth flashed white when he smiled. Then he dropped a silk stovepipe hat on his head and, towering over two policemen, strode the rest of the way to Rittenhouse Square. The knees of his trousers were stained with mud.

Mr. Schneider brought us back at four o'clock, long before the opera let out and the Pryces got home. Clarissa did not say a blessed word about where we had spent the afternoon. It was two years later when Mr. Lincoln returned to Philadelphia before Mrs. Pryce found out. She asked Clarissa if she would care to see President Lincoln.

"Oh, we've met him," Clarissa answered, tossing her curls. "Me and Hitty both."

I remember so well the day old Grandfather Pryce walked in and said to Clarissa's mother, "Sarah, war has broken out between North and South. Our country will be torn apart."

Quakers did not believe that anything was worth killing other people about. Quakers didn't send men away to fight, but we all felt the war keenly. Many a time I sat on the front steps or watched from a window with Clarissa as lines of men in blue tunics marched by, guns on their shoulders, their feet all moving like the spokes of wheels, till it made us dizzy. The man who drove the Pryce's carriage, the lad who groomed the horses, and the young man who sold us fresh groceries from his wagon all disappeared from regular life into the war like water swirling down a drain.

Ruth knitted socks and sent them to the boys she knew best. There was one, John Norton, who sent her a button from his first uniform and also a picture of himself. She treasured both very carefully. Ruth was quieter than she had been a year ago. It turned out that she had promised John Norton to marry him when he came back from fighting in the swamps of Louisiana.

By this time Clarissa was almost thirteen and paid less attention to me than before. Each evening she helped the women who gathered to make bandages for the wounded soldiers. I sat in my corner of the living room mantelpiece and watched them at it.

In a letter Ruth heard that John Norton was seriously wounded.

"Ruth's worried sick he won't ever come

back," Clarissa said to me. "She wears the button he gave her on a ribbon round her neck, and she sleeps with his letters under her pillow. I saw her put them there the other night."

Clarissa was sent away to Quaker boarding school the third year of the war, and I only saw her on holidays. She gave away the rag and china babies, but she kept me, even though she declared she was too old for dolls. I lost track of time again, and the sounds of drums and fifes in the street outside stirred me no more than the ticking of the clock in the hall.

I told myself that when the war was over everything would be as it had been before. But I knew better than to believe this, for a doll of my experience has learned that nothing can ever be just the same once there has been change of any sort.

Another letter came from John Norton, who was better and being cared for in a Georgia hospital.

"There is a little girl here who brings me flowers sometimes," he wrote Ruth. "She is a year or two younger than Clarissa, and she has a doll with a cloth head because the china one got shot away when her house was under fire. Her name is Camilla Calhoun and she likes to have me tell her about Clarissa's doll, Hitty. Today she brought me forget-me-not flowers and said, 'Send them to the Yankee doll.' So here they are."

In the letter was a crumple of petals and leaves. It was Ruth who packed me off then and there to that little southern girl who needed a doll and had been kind to John Norton way down south in Georgia. ★

CHAPTER TEN
I Go to War

 Y WOODEN BOX was well made. Ruth had sewn an inch-long American flag to the bosom of my dress. She took care to cushion me in wads of cotton batting. Because of this wadding it was diffi-cult to hear all that was going on around me, but I'd heard enough of war for one doll's lifetime, no matter how many years I live to tell my adventures.

Sending a parcel through the enemy lines was no easy thing in wartime. I got only as far as a Rebel army post office in Charleston, South Carolina. There I was opened by Sergeant Jim Chapelle, who thought I might be some sort of a gun-powder canister sent from Philadelphia to blow them up. When he unpacked me I thought his eyes would pop right out of his head. Then he laughed in relief and set me on the post office windowsill for all the boys to see.

"A Yankee doll, for sure," he explained to one and all, "but she's a touch of home.

I aim to send her along to Georgia when the fighting dies down and it's safe to get a package through."

When you live on one side of a war, everybody says the other side is good for nothing on this earth. Otherwise it wouldn't be nice to shoot them. To hear the talk in Philadelphia, the rebels in the South were a mob of scoundrels. The ones I met in Carolina were just plain farm boys. None but the officers owned a decent pair of shoes, and they all wrote home to their mammas and pappas.

So many rebel boys came from deep and far in the mountains. They had never set foot in a schoolhouse and couldn't write more than an *X* to sign their names. They spoke their letters to Sergeant Jim, and he wrote them out and sent them.

Jim Chapelle put an officer's epaulet tab on the front of my dress to cover my Yankee flag. The soldiers saluted me when they came in to look for their letters. From the limestone windowsill in the one-room post office, I looked out on Magnolia Street. The dogwoods bloomed and turned to leaf. Children raced out of their houses to play. Dogs barked, and life looked not too different from life in Philadelphia. I had my eye on one small girl who reminded me of Phoebe Preble. Every morning she walked her collie dog past my window and waved at me. I hoped she would ask Sergeant Jim if she could take me home, because I had lost all hope of ever being delivered to Camilla Calhoun.

Whoever my friend with the collie dog was I will never know, because the post office was blown up on the morning of February 17, 1865. You could feel the thump of Yankee cannon shelling the city. Families poured into the streets and left their homes to burn. My box with Camilla Calhoun's Georgia address on it was buried under a ton of rubble and I would have been matchsticks if I hadn't been left on the limestone windowsill. Jim Chapelle disappeared. All my new friends in gray coats melted away like April snow, and in their place came other soldiers in blue.

The post office roof was gone. All three other walls were gone. The whole of Magnolia Street was a wreck of collapsed houses.

I sat in the rain and sun. My Quaker-gray dress faded. My epaulet tab fell off, and the tiny flag sewn to my shirtfront drained to pink and lavender. Never did I think I would belong to anyone ever again. ✦

CHAPTER ELEVEN

I Am Put to Use

 NE DAY A carriage stopped at what remained of the post office. A plump and no-nonsense lady got out. She saw me, plucked me from my sill, and sat me down next to her in her carriage. Her name was Mary Chesnut. She was smart and proud and she loved her big family.

"Hitty," she said when she'd taken off my old dress and read the cross-stitched name on my camisole. "Hitty, I think you have been well loved."

Mary Chesnut asked Millie Nettletree, her seamstress, to make me a flannel nightgown. Mary Chesnut placed me on her writing table. At night she talked to me about how the war had broken her family and her heart. As she talked she wrote her

hopes and worries down in a diary that must have been a thousand pages long.

I didn't know for the longest time when the war was really over. I suppose my Philadelphia friends were joyful, but the city of Charleston was a pile of ashes, and no one there had anything to eat or a roof over their heads. I might have stayed propped up on Mary's table into the next century. I could have been a permanent part of her big family, if it had not been for Millie.

Millie Nettletree was an ex-slave, and she had other plans for me. She had taught herself to read with no schooling. She'd sewn clothing good enough for the governor and his wife with one rusty steel sewing needle, which she kept safely in a velvet-lined box as if it were made of gold.

I served as Mrs. Chesnut's dress model. All patterns were tried out on me first. One morning Millie appeared at Mrs. Chesnut's house, ready to make a dress out of bedroom draperies. Nothing could be bought in the shops at the time.

"Look at this, Mrs. Chesnut," said Millie as she pulled out a newspaper and began to read aloud. "A one-hundred-dollar cash prize will be given to the winner of the New Orleans Cotton Exposition Contest. Mrs. Chesnut, if I could win this hundred dollars I'd have enough money to send my granddaughter, Parthenia, to the Young Ladies' Academy and buy her school books."

Mrs. Chesnut read the advertisement for herself. "If anyone can win this contest,

Millie, you can," she said. "I will lend you Hitty and my own wedding necklace of black pearls to make her the prizewinning outfit. Something good should come of this war."

Millie brought me to a home no bigger than my one-room post office. She had few possessions, but there was a bookcase with two precious books in it. Millie slept on folded army blankets in the corner. By the light of her one lamp, which was a cotton wick in a sea shell of oil, she looked very fierce. Her mouth bristled with pins, and her hands snip-snipped Mrs. Chesnut's silver scissors for days and nights in a row.

"Don't like these old red beads. Don't like this creature in the middle with the little bitty gold eyes one bit!" muttered Millie. I was horrified. She tried to snip through my coral and elephant-head necklace, but the silver scissors balked and would not cut through the fishing line.

"It doesn't exactly go with the dress," Mrs. Chesnut said later. "Hide it under a high collar, Millie. It's hers, after all."

New needles came in to the shops at last, and I was soon in a dress that looked like a snowy wonderland.

Millie sewed slippers soft as milkweed pods for me with stitches so small I could hardly see them. She made a wreath for my hair out of ribbons and pearls, and a veil so delicate spiders might have woven it by moonlight. One by one she lined up more luminous teardrop pearls and sewed them into a pattern of lily petals on the front of my dress.

All the time Millie chattered to me. "You are going to make a difference, little Yankee doll," she said. "You are going to get my granddaughter, Parthenia, enough book learning so she can rise up in this terrible world. Then some fine day her little girl can eat cream cakes and play with dolls."

What a chance, I thought, for a doll not just to be loved and admired, but to be part of changing someone's world. ✦

CHAPTER TWELVE

I Go on Exhibition

HE CITY HALL of New Orleans looked like a toy shop. Dolls in every possible kind of clothing were lined up in the mayor's office. The mayor's wife and her sisters were the judges of the contest. Some dolls were French with china heads and hands, real hair and glass eyes. I was reminded of the dolls that shamed Thankful and me in Janet Pryce's house so long ago. But those who fail at first sometimes shine in the end. Millie Nettletree's artistry won me the first prize hands down. I watched one hundred dollars go into a beautiful buff envelope sealed with the mayor's seal and wax. Off it went in the mail to Millie. I could not wait to get back to Charleston and see how well Parthenia Nettletree would do.

But first I had to be on exhibition and let the whole city and all its visitors admire me. I was put in a glass case. The lock on the door was fastened with a gold key kept in a guard's pocket.

I must have seen hundreds of people go by. One little girl came several times to look me over. She was about eight, I guessed, and she carried a shop-worn parasol.

Her father wore a coat like a sea captain's. "Sally, come on now," he wheedled at her. He could never get her to leave at closing time, and in the morning she was back again, memorizing every detail of my dress and me.

Nothing escaped her sharp eyes. That's how she got her chance.

The guard noticed rain blowing in an open window one evening. When he went to close it he left the key in my lock for two minutes. Sally crept over to my case. She looked quickly all around, then turned the key with steady fingers. The door swung open and her hand darted in and seized me firmly about the waist. I felt myself being stuffed into the red silk umbrella.

Only too well I knew the sounds and smells of dockyards. This is where the swinging umbrella took me. We boarded the *Morning-Glory*, a river steamboat that ran between New Orleans and the upper Mississippi bringing bales of cotton down south and taking other cargoes on the return trip up north. I wanted to go home to Charleston, I wanted to see how Parthenia Nettletree did in her school, and I wanted to belong to Mary Chesnut's grandchildren. But dolls have not much choice in the world and, just as accidentally as Phoebe Preble dropped me in a gutter in India, I belonged to a captain's daughter again.

Naturally I couldn't show my face on deck or in the open because I was stolen

property. Sally kept me hidden on a shelf where she could talk to me and where I had a good view of the brown waters of the Mississippi River. I don't think anyone had given her a doll before. Her mother, I believe, was dead and she was a lonely girl, not used to playing much of anything.

The captain made frequent stops to deliver cargoes along the way. I think it was at Natchez, a fine city of wharves and much pleasant greenery, that I heard Captain Loomis read a notice about me in the newspaper.

"Come here, Sally, and listen to this," I heard him say as they sat on deck near our cabin. "It's all about that doll you took such a shine to at the Cotton Show." And he began to read aloud from the paper:

MYSTERIOUS DISAPPEARANCE OF DOLL AT COTTON EXPOSITION
Unexplained theft of valuable exhibit from glass case — Prizewinning workmanship with heirloom pearls. Police at work on all clues — Reward offered.

"Well, now, what do you think of that?" And he chuckled under his beard.

But Sally made no answer.

"Let's see," her father went on, without noticing this. "Disappeared yesterday afternoon, and this paper's three days old. Why, that was the very day you were there. She wasn't gone then, was she?"

"No, I saw her," Sally managed to reply.

It was the truth, but I could not help wondering what her father would say if he knew that I sat within earshot of him at that very moment.

"Seems it was only loaned to the exposition," he went on as he read, "and they're real worked up over it. The man in charge of the room says he left for just a minute. When he got back the key was in the lock same's he'd left it, only the doll was gone

73

and not a soul in sight. He gave the alarm and they started searching everyone in the place, but there wasn't so much as a sign of it."

There was another long silence before I heard Sally's voice again.

"Pa," she said, "what would they do to anybody who took the doll? I mean, if they found out who did?"

"Do?" said the captain. "Oh, I expect what they always do to thieves—lock 'em up in jail. Well, it's lucky we went there when we did so's you could see the doll."

In her cabin Sally took me out very carefully and hugged me tight.

"I don't care what that old newspaper says," she whispered in sudden defiance. "I won't give you back, and they won't catch me, either."

Out my porthole I caught glimpses of cotton or sugarcane fields where people were at work, of moss-hung live oaks, of white-pillared houses behind tall trees and gardens. I longed to see more of this river panorama so new to me.

One Sunday I got my chance. Captain Loomis brought the *Morning-Glory* up to a rickety old wharf. No one paid any attention to Sally and me. Once ashore she took me out and carried me around openly, as if she had come by me honestly.

The sun blazed hot on the cabins and the frame church. People carried big palm-leaf fans and bunches of flowers, and some had tiny babies in their arms. Sally and I followed them and sat with other children on a board placed across two molasses kegs. It was even hotter in the church than outside. The babies whimpered. Flies droned in spite of the waving fans. The man in the pulpit grew shinier and shinier on his bald head as he talked. I can remember only a little of what he said, but there was one part that made a great impression on Sally.

"My sisters and brethren," he began, "I am going to tell you about the eighth commandment. The eighth commandment tells us 'Thou shalt not steal.' Don't you imagine, my brethren, that you can go on fooling the Lord forever, because He's got His eye right on you and there ain't the smallest child here that He ain't able to look right down into his heart and see if there's sin hidden there."

I could feel Sally stiffen at his words. She sat with her eyes fixed on his face. I knew what she was thinking. She did not join in the singing of hymns—instead she sat quiet in her place. It was only after everyone trooped out behind the preacher to follow him down to the river that she rose and went slowly after them.

The preacher urged everyone who wanted to have his sins washed away to come out to him in waist-high water.

"Glory, glory, glory!" the preacher shouted. "Another soul is saved!"

Everyone had been too busy to notice the immense thundercaps rolling up. The sudden rumble of thunder sent the whole congregation scuttling to shelter. From their looks of panic I guess they connected the storm with the preacher's warnings.

Sally ran in the opposite direction, toward the landing where the *Morning-Glory* was tied up. The sky was a purplish color, and jagged forks of lightning began to rip through it. The cottonwood trees looked ghostly in the strange light. I could feel Sally shiver.

Crash! A tree went down a few yards ahead of us with a splintering sound I had not heard since the topmast had shattered on the *Diana-Kate*.

"Dear God," Sally wailed, "don't let the lightning strike me dead, please! I'll give Hitty back. I won't keep her another minute, Lord—look, here she is. You can have her, only just let me get back to Pa and the *Morning-Glory*!"

Now she was running down the bank toward the river. I knew only too well what she meant to do with me. ✦

CHAPTER THIRTEEN
I Come to Live on a Plantation

 OSES WAS NOT the only one set to float on a river in a basket. But if I remember the story rightly from my days with Thankful's family in India, his sister kept a very careful watch over him.

In time I came to rest. It was not among bulrushes but between the wooden piles of an old landing, and I was fished up not by a princess of Egypt but by a couple of boys out fishing in a flat-bottomed boat. The small one decided they might as well take me back to his little sister Caroline. They had no intention, however, of letting me interfere with their fishing. I lay on my back in the bottom of the boat among a tangle of fish line and a string of slimy, flopping fish.

Toward sundown, the boys took their catch home. They each lived with brothers and sisters in the cabins behind some ancient, moss-draped live oaks. It seemed to be part of a huge cotton plantation. As far as the eye could see were even rows of white puff balls.

"She's mine!" Caroline said, as proudly as if I had been in the richest of silks instead of my brown-stained, fish-spoiled dress.

Their mother made good and sure Caroline's brother had found me honestly. She seemed afraid he would be punished if anyone came looking for me. But Caroline was so happy to have me that her mother did not have the heart to take me away.

The cabin was too small for all the children and grown-ups who had to sleep in it every night. But what it had not in room it made up for in much love. At least the weather was warm enough to allow one to sit outdoors all year. In the evenings grown-ups and children sat outside cooking around a big open fire. I liked to hear them sing. Their sad voices were sweeter than those of any children I had ever met before.

Caroline made me a house out of an orange crate, wallpapered with the flowered pages of a seed catalogue. Someone made me a bed out of Sally's wicker basket, and a chair and table out of twigs. Caroline and her friends had never had enough money to own anything more than a few clothes. The girls from other cabins took turns holding me. I think Caroline must have grown up to be a business woman of great success. She allowed her friends to play with me if they would contribute to

my wardrobe or my house. Soon I owned ten dresses of calico and taffeta scraps. The walls of my orange crate had framed bits of mirror, rugs, blankets, and even a tiny candlestick with a candle made by her best friend, Sarah, in the next cabin. I had never been so well provided for in all my days.

Sarah's older sister, Hope, from New Orleans, came visiting at Christmas. Sarah dragged her big sister by the hand to come around and see me in Caroline's house. I had a Christmas tree of a pine sprig. On top was a gold star cut from the wrapping on a box of sugar.

Hope studied me sitting in my finery. Something told me this was one of the moments that change a person's life forever. I thought I remembered her face from somewhere. She had once seen me before, I knew that. "Where did you get her?" she asked.

Caroline told her about her brother fishing me out of the river.

"Did she have another dress on then?" Hope asked.

Caroline brought out the dress Millie Nettletree had made.

"Why," said Hope, grabbing Caroline by the shoulders and shaking her, "I recognize this doll from the Cotton Exposition in New Orleans last year. These are real pearls and there's a five-hundred-dollar reward for her if anybody gives her back."

"But Hitty's mine," said Caroline in a testy voice.

"Caroline," answered Hope, "think of it this way. Five hundred dollars is going to buy your daddy and mamma a new house you all can fit into and ten dolls with real hair and satin gowns for you and all your friends!" ✦

CHAPTER FOURTEEN

I Sit for a Portrait

T WAS THE pearls everyone was after, of course. They couldn't have cared a bit about me.

Hope was given the $500 reward for Caroline. Her smiling picture was in the newspaper. As for me, they took Millie Nettletree's pearl-studded dress off and sent it back to Mrs. Chesnut. I was placed in a storeroom for unclaimed merchandise in the New Orleans city hall.

There were two other unreturned contest dolls with lost addresses in the closet. Both of them were fancy and French, Hortense and Violette. This is a very rough translation of their opinions:

"Without her prizewinning dress this American doll is nothing," was Hortense's.

"She was nothing even when she was wearing the pearly dress, dear sister," was Violette's. "And without the pearls her dress was nothing, too!"

They considered their language superior to English and were not interested in learning a single word. It took me years to learn to follow what they said. But, then, it was better than being stuffed in a sofa.

I thought I might end up seeing the beginning of the next century in this dusky storeroom when one day the wife of the mayor of New Orleans looked in.

"Humph," she said. "This one will have to do."

She picked up Hortense.

"I hate that doll, Grandma," said a voice behind her.

"Well then, this one," said her grandmother.

"I hate that one, too."

"This little wooden one is the only other one and she hasn't a stitch on her body," said Grandmother.

"I want my zebra in my lap," said the little girl.

"Nonsense," said her grandmother. "You are having your portrait painted by Mr. John Singleton Copley the third. His grandfather painted George Washington and you will have a doll, not a zebra, in your lap. I'll put one of the French dolls' dresses on this little wooden one. Look, her name is written here in cross stitch. It's *Hitty*. I'll shorten the dress myself to fit her and that's the end of that."

"I hate all dolls," said her granddaughter, having the last word.

I must admit to smiling as I came out of the storeroom in a blue-and-white striped silk shirtwaist, leaving behind my superior French friend, naked as a jaybird.

I had never met a little girl who hated dolls, but Isabella Van Rensselaer certainly did. She went to bed surrounded by bears and lions and her precious zebra, Zazu. I was put on a bookshelf.

Mr. John Singleton Copley thought differently. He admired me from the start. "Hitty is a beauty all right," he said. "Made by a real artist, she was. Close to a century old judging from the wear and tear she's had. Oh, what stories I bet this doll could tell!"

Isabella's portrait took weeks to paint because Isabella was not a good sitter. Sitting still was no hardship at all for me, but Isabella fretted on the slub silk settee and sprang up at the slightest excuse. She was as permanently messy as any boy. Her hair swirled into whorls and ringlets before the hairbrush was put down. She came untucked as soon as her grandmother straightened her skirts. Her socks squirreled themselves down in her shoes, and her shoes flew across the room the moment she kicked her feet.

The instant Mr. Copley was finished with the oil painting, Isabella tore outside and climbed up a tree. She sat in the crotch of a large branch and looked in the window, hair ribbon gone, all covered with pine sap. "You can't get me!" she said, laughing.

"I wish I had such a nice doll as Hitty to pose with all my subjects," said Mr. Copley, eyeing me.

84

"You are welcome to her," said Isabella's grandmother. "This child hates dolls and will probably feed Hitty to one of her stuffed lions."

"She'll grow out of it," Mr. Copley assured Isabella's grandmother.

The grandmother looked out the window at Isabella, who was traveling from branch to branch like a monkey. "I think not," she answered.

Isabella may not have liked me, but all the same I liked her and I was sorry I never had the opportunity to say a proper good-bye to her.

Mr. Copley packed me in his comfortable leather bag. In his hotel room he examined my paint. It had chipped and worn off and what was left of my expression was soft and dreamy.

"You're a beautiful girl, Hitty," said Mr. Copley, "but you've seen a bit of the world and everyone needs a little help from time to time."

Oh, if only I could have told him that I had been held in the hand that wrote the Gettysburg Address.

Mr. Copley was careful to use just the right colors. He followed the peddler's brush strokes exactly. When he was finished he held me up in front of the mirror so I could see the blush on my cheeks, my sparkling eyes, and my rosy mouth as I had not seen them since I'd fallen off the deck of the *Diana-Kate*. When I had dried we went to paint the next portrait of a little rich girl or boy.

And the next.

And the next.

Until we found ourselves northward bound on the Southern Crescent train. Mr. Copley let me look out the window. He propped me up next to his dinner in the dining car and talked to me.

"I'm not the famous painter Grandfather Copley was, Hitty," he said. "No indeed. Grandfather would turn over in his grave if he saw me living hand-to-mouth in hotels and painting the spoiled rich children of spoiled rich mothers."

Mr. Copley finished his soup. The waiter brought chops. "Oh, but my next customers, Hitty! This job could put me on the map. And it's all because America's most famous painter, snooty Mr. John 'Stuffed-Shirt' Sargent, refused the job!"

The train came to a stop at Chattanooga Station.

"And why did America's most famous artist refuse this particular job?" Mr. Copley asked me while cutting a lamb chop. "Because," he answered for me, "these particular children would not behave for a minute and their father made more trouble than all six children put together! So we have our work cut out for us, my girl!"

After three days on the train we alighted at Union Station, Washington, D.C.

When we arrived at the east-wing door of the big house, none of the children could be found. All afternoon their mother flushed them out of their hiding places, only to see them climb a drain spout or jump from chair to bed to sofa. Their father did nothing but laugh and encourage them. He got down on his hands and knees and made horse whinnies for his youngest boy, Quentin. There were two girls, one proper older one, Alice, and Ethel, who was as wild as her brothers.

I got to know them quite well. I sat in Ethel's lap every day while Mr. Copley painted. The boys brought their badgers and bunnies and even their pony, General Grant, inside the White House rooms. Their mother, Mrs. Roosevelt, shooed him out and scolded Quentin for getting hoof marks on the waxed floors.

"I'd rather have a muddy scuff from a pony than the oily boot heels of most members of the Congress!" trumpeted Mr. Roosevelt.

I have seen many fathers in my days on earth as a doll, but he was the best of all because he was really there.

Theodore Roosevelt was too lively for Mr. Copley to include in the painting. Mrs. Roosevelt was too busy organizing her brood to sit still either. But someday, if you are ever in the National Gallery in Washington, D.C., you will find the Roosevelt children's portrait. There's Alice, very grown-up, and Ted with the glasses like his father, and Kermit, Archie, and Quentin. Look hard and you'll see me in the folds of eleven-year-old Ethel's lap. I am wearing Hortense's blue-and-white-striped shirtwaist. Ethel's right hand just covers my feet.

I thought I might end my days as a White House mascot, or at least at Sagamore Hill as a member of the enormous Roosevelt

clan, but it was not in the cards. I went north again to Boston with Mr. Copley. The Roosevelt children's portrait won him the fame and fortune he so much wanted. We painted Vanderbilt children, and Rockefeller children, and some big Irish family in Hyannisport whose name I have forgotten, but they were even wilder children than the Roosevelts. We charged more and more for every painting. ★

CHAPTER FIFTEEN

I Receive an Education

R. COPLEY RECEIVED a letter from New York. He read it to me aloud.

Dear Mr. Copley,   *November 20, 1925*

My family had the pleasure of seeing your excellent portrait of the Roosevelt children, presently in our National Gallery. My daughter Rebecca was so taken with it that she asked to go back every day of our visit to Washington. As it happens she seems to have fallen in love with the small doll in young Ethel Roosevelt's lap.

After much letter writing I discovered that the doll is a model and belongs to you. My daughter has asked me to invite you to tea here in

Brooklyn, should you ever come to New York for a portrait. Please do accept and bring your model for Rebecca to meet. (If at all possible, her birthday is December 4.)

Enclosed is her picture.

Yours truly,
Nathan Solomon

Mr. Copley stared at the photo a long minute. Then he showed it to me. Rebecca Solomon looked like any other little girl, smiley and dark-haired, but she sat in a chair that held her legs in straps and buckles.

"Well, Hitty, what do you think?" Mr. Copley asked me. "December fourth is next week. I wasn't planning to go to New York for anything."

In the secret way that dolls speak, I told him.

In the secret way that very sensitive people listen, Mr. Copley heard me.

"You've brought me wonderful luck, my girl," he said and got out a packing crate. "Let's see if you can bring luck to young Rebecca."

★ ★ ★

Rebecca's laugh on opening my birthday paper wrapping was like spring sunshine after a long, cold winter, and if I'd been able to laugh, my laugh would have matched hers. I had not belonged to a little girl since Caroline, because I don't count doll-hating Isabella. The moment I laid eyes on her I knew I would have to try to bring her luck. But what is the power of mountain ash against an illness that didn't have a name? Her legs wouldn't walk and that was the beginning and end of it as far as I could see. But her father and mother adored her and that was the most important thing.

In the evening the first thing Mr. Solomon did was lift his daughter out of her chair and swing her high in the air. He was not as big a man as Captain Preble, but then Rebecca weighed no more than a bird.

Mr. Solomon was a tailor, Rebecca explained to me. "Daddy dresses dukes and dandies," she said. "He makes the snazziest suits in New York City."

Snazzy was a new word for me.

"Give me a Wall Street jelly-belly," Mr. Solomon used to say, "and I'll make him look like the Prince of Wales."

The secret was in the vest. He put in whalebone stays like a woman's corset and pulled in saggy old business men's stomachs like magic.

"Tummy trim for the tycoons" was his motto. Mr. Solomon worked six days a week to support his family and afford the finer things in life. He never appeared without a polka-dot bow tie and a flower in his lapel.

Rebecca did not let me leave her lap or pillow, and she did not stop smiling after her birthday. In those days people in wheelchairs

were kept at home. Rebecca's mother taught her every-thing. I believe that in this way Mrs. Solomon, Rebecca, and I learned more about the world than most people who have gone around it three times.

After his morning Ovaltine Mr. Solomon kissed Mrs. Solomon on both cheeks and Rebecca on both cheeks and said, "You're in charge, Hitty!"

Our schoolbook was the daily paper, *The New York Herald*. Rebecca recited every inch of it aloud, including the crossword and the Hollywood gossip. She made charts all over her walls of weather patterns, the price of gold in London, and how the Brooklyn Dodgers were doing. No one could sneeze from Argentina to Zanzibar without us knowing about it.

In the afternoons Rebecca read me stories from ten different colored books of fairy tales. She made up plays about all the characters. For these plays Rebecca sewed me special costumes. I was King Arthur in tinfoil, Buffalo Bill in fringed chamois cloth, or the Lady of the Lake floating up in the goldfish bowl.

Rebecca would have gone on very happily the way she was if it hadn't been for Aunt Edna and the Crash.

I didn't hear any crash. I must have been asleep or too far away to notice it, but people certainly talked about it. First all the neighbors lost their money and jobs. It was the end of the tummy-tucked tycoons. Within a year Mr. Solomon's shop had to close and he was selling elevator shoes door-to-door. No one in the whole of Brooklyn could afford the finer things in life.

"Rose," said Aunt Edna one afternoon, "Rebecca needs to be in school with other children her age."

"She can't, Edna, you know that. She's not well."

"She's certainly not going to get well if she goes on like this," said Aunt Edna. "There's a boarding school upstate that takes kids in wheelchairs, on crutches, you name it. These people have a heated pool. They'll help Rebecca walk again. Just think about it, Rose. Don't say anything, just think about it."

Rebecca's eyes filled with tears. She hugged me tight. "I don't want to go, Hitty," she said. "I don't want to go to any boarding school."

Mrs. Solomon did not bring the subject up at all. I thought it had gone with the wind, but that was not the end of Aunt Edna.

The next time she visited she brought a brochure from the boarding school.

"We can't afford it, Edna," said Rebecca's mother. "Nate says it's too expensive."

"Sell something, Rose," said Edna. "We're talking about your child's health and education. Sell Mother's sterling silver tea service. It's worth a mint."

"I'm not carrying Mother's tea service through the streets like some pushcart vendor in the old country, Edna," said Mrs. Solomon.

Aunt Edna brought a man named Mr. D'Ardsley from the secondhand shop up to our apartment. He turned over the teapot and the creamer and the sugar tongs and shook his head. "Plate," he said. "Dime a dozen, Mrs. Solomon. It's not sterling and it's not worth the metal it's made of. Ten dollars, I'm afraid, is the best I can do."

I could feel Rebecca's happy heart pounding in her chest. "No boarding school," she said under her breath. "No boarding school."

For once Aunt Edna was speechless. But just as Mr. D'Ardsley said good-bye and how sorry he was, he put on his glasses again and looked at me.

"Now there you've got something," he said.

"Hitty?" asked Rebecca's mother.

"Show the man Hitty, Rebecca," said Aunt Edna.

"Probably about 1820," he said, examining me carefully. "Beautiful. A rare piece of Americana. Give you a nice price for her."

"She's mine and she's not for sale," said Rebecca and she snatched me back and slammed the door of the bedroom behind us.

Rebecca was twelve then. She was old enough to wheel her own chair out the door and into the street and down to the public library. She did this at three-thirty every day of the week.

Aunt Edna knew it. One day at exactly four o'clock Aunt Edna let herself into the apartment on tiptoe. She sneaked into Rebecca's bedroom and stuffed me in her bag.

"That child will thank me one day," I heard Aunt Edna mutter. I could only hope this would prove true. If going to boarding school would help Rebecca stand up and walk and make some friends, then her heart and mine would not be so broken after all. This, of course, is the way a doll must think when leaving an owner whose life takes a separate path. ✦

CHAPTER SIXTEEN
I Come to Live in the Shop of Dreams

R. D'ARDSLEY'S STORE was a pawn shop. On the window were the words SHOP OF DREAMS. All of the objects inside had loan tickets, but if no one came to reclaim their property after a time, things went on sale.

Behind me in the window was an Italian violin. A musician had brought it in for twenty-five dollars when his orchestra closed down. Around me ran an electric train. It had belonged to a banker's son. All their money was lost in the terrible Crash and they got five dollars for the train.

There were tin trucks, bronze bookends, and a stuffed Gila monster. There were no other dolls, but I did have some company. It was Mr. Abraham Lincoln. He had been made into an iron money bank. He popped up and doffed his hat when a penny was put in the slot. Just from his expression I could tell Lincoln thought this was very undignified for a president.

Some evenings I noticed an old lady with white hair walk slowly by. She never failed to gaze in the window. I came to look forward to her beading eyes on me.

Finally she came in the shop.

Mr. D'Ardsley asked her, "May I help you?"

She rubbed her cold hands together over the shop's small heater. "I'd like to see that doll . . . the little one over there."

Mr. D'Ardsley plucked me out of the window display.

She held me and smiled. "I notice her necklace," the old lady said. "The coral beads and the elephant with the pinpoint gold eyes. There couldn't be but one of these in the world."

Startled by her comment, I tried to get a better look at her. Something about her eyes looked familiar, but, then, I had a hundred years of faces to remember.

"She's one of a kind," agreed Mr. D'Ardsley. "Have you seen her before?"

"Not me. Not me," answered the old lady.

My admirer stopped often on her way home from work. She always asked to look at me. Times were hard and business was slow. Mr. D'Ardsley was lonely and I noticed he'd begin fussing about five o'clock and make a pot of cocoa in the hope that she'd stop by. She usually did. But those two were shy with each other.

"May I ask you something, sir?" the old lady said one rainy night, stirring sugar into her chocolate.

"Of course."

"Would it be improper to ask you to take the blue-striped dress off this doll? Is there a shirt underneath with stitching on it?"

Delicately Mr. D'Ardsley undressed me. "Yes," he said, "as a matter of fact there is."

"Let me think now. Don't tell me. Does that stitching say 'H-I-T-T-Y'?"

"So it does," he answered. "How on earth did you know that?"

Yes, how did *she* know that? I wondered.

"How much does she cost?" asked the old lady.

Mr. D'Ardsley told her and she shook her head.

"Well," she said, "I'm just a schoolteacher and I can't afford that. But I collect my classroom library fines each week and I could put those toward her."

Mr. D'Ardsley placed his hands on the desk. "I will take your installments, ma'am," he answered, "but if a customer comes along and offers full price I will have to sell her and refund your money in full. Otherwise I can't pay the rent for the store."

"That sounds right to me," said the old lady. "I'll come back Wednesday with my next payment."

People tell both everything and nothing to dolls. Sometimes it takes forever for us to find out the simplest thing. You can imagine how curious I was to know how this woman knew what name was in cross-stitch on my camisole.

On the day of her tenth weekly payment she sat down in the back of the shop and, being slightly less shy, asked Mr. D'Ardsley his name.

He told her and asked her to tell him her name in return.

"Oh, of course," she answered. "It's Miss Parthenia Nettletree."

Mr. D'Ardsley wrote it down in his ledger and poured her a cup of chocolate.

It was Millie Nettletree's quicksilver eyes from a lifetime ago that I had recognized in Parthenia, Millie's granddaughter. Her grandmother would have been so proud. Parthenia had not a great deal of money, but she had been given her books and her schooling and was teaching others; and in this were more riches than any money could buy.

At this very moment I still sit in the window of the Shop of Dreams. My days here are not dull. Each new customer who enters the shop fills me with interest and suspense. Who knows but this may be the one who carries me away to further adventures? I feel that many more are awaiting me. Just the other morning I heard a curious purring noise high in the air and saw what appeared to be a gigantic dragonfly with silvery wings swooping and sporting in the blue sky.

"Oh, see the airplane?" cried a little child out on the sidewalk. "I'd like to fly in one someday."

I watched it fly out of sight with a sense of wonder. Perhaps, like the child on the sidewalk, I, too, shall take to the air. Why not, since the world is always arranging new experiences for us, and I have never felt more hale and hearty in my life? After all, what is a century or two to well-seasoned mountain ash? ✦

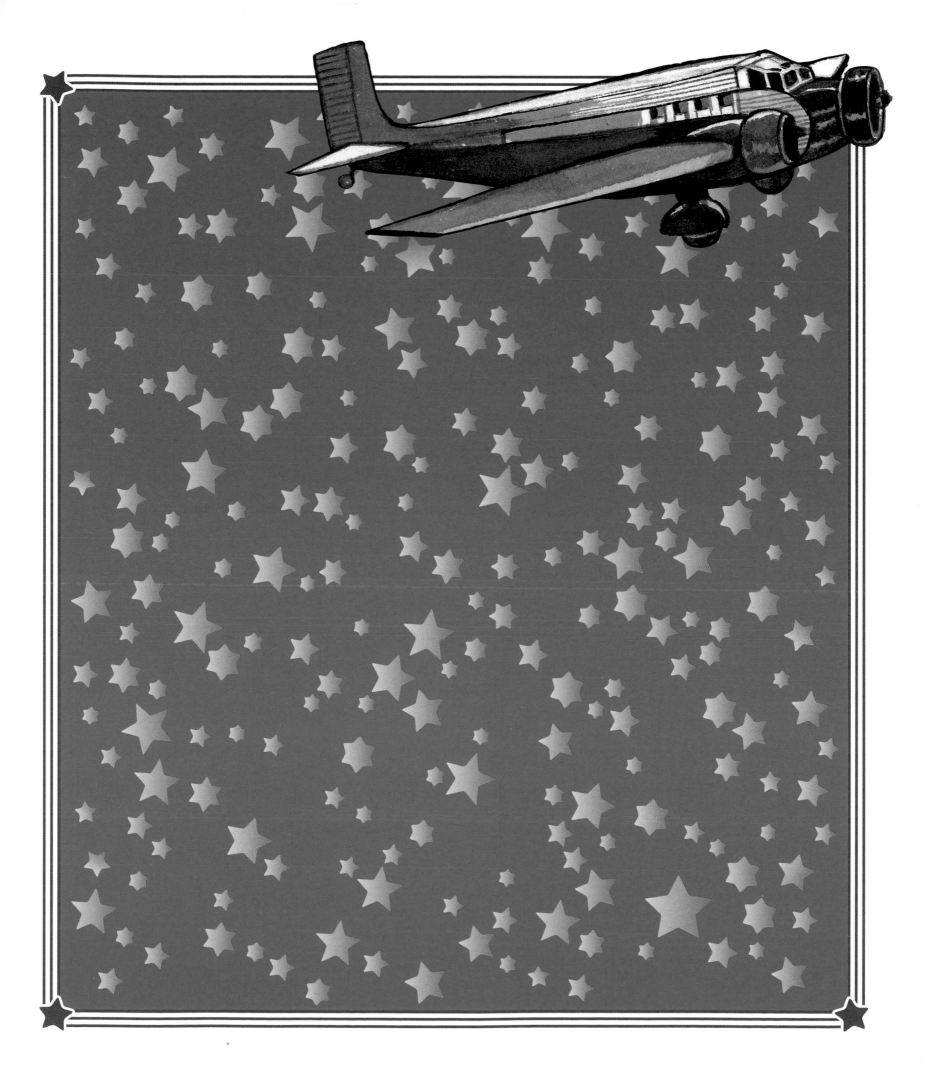

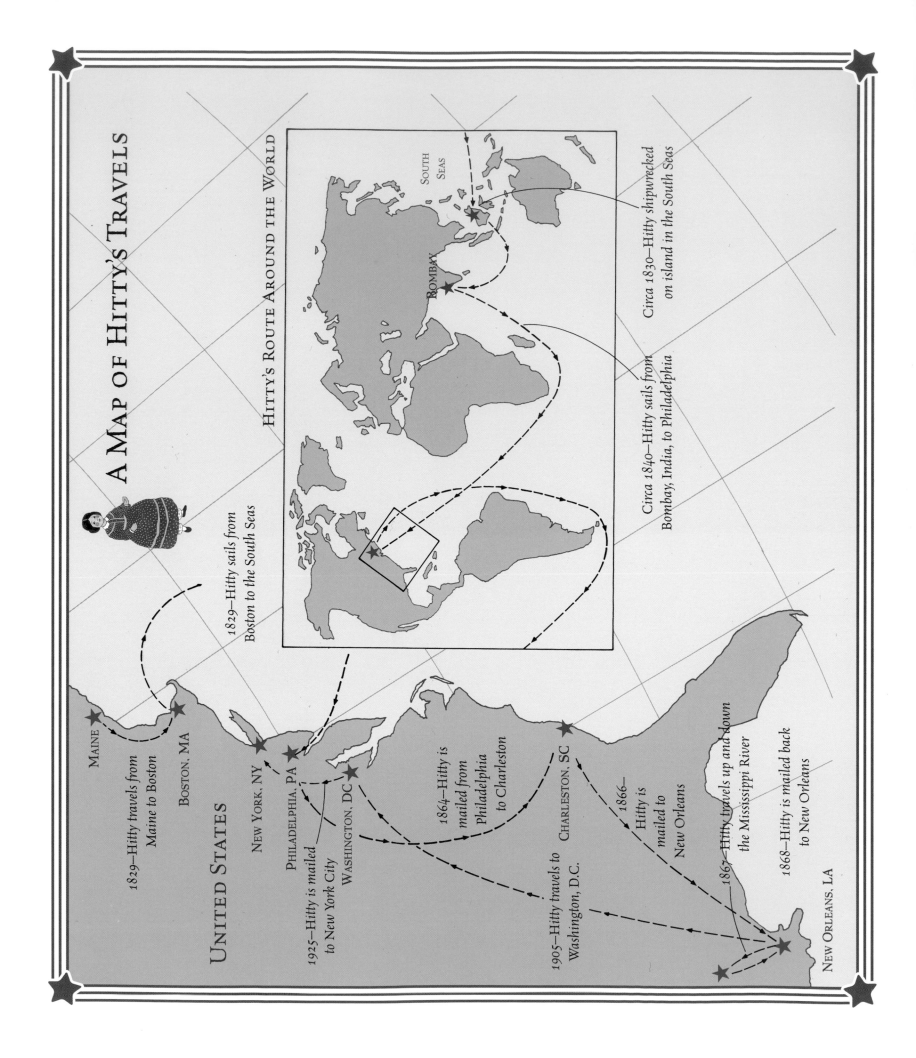

A Map of Hitty's Travels

United States

Maine

1829—Hitty travels from Maine to Boston

Boston, MA

New York, NY

Philadelphia, PA

1925—Hitty is mailed to New York City

Washington, D.C.

1905—Hitty travels to Washington, D.C.

1864—Hitty is mailed from Philadelphia to Charleston

Charleston, SC

1866—Hitty is mailed to New Orleans

1867—Hitty travels up and down the Mississippi River

1868—Hitty is mailed back to New Orleans

New Orleans, LA

Hitty's Route Around the World

1829—Hitty sails from Boston to the South Seas

South Seas

Bombay

Circa 1830—Hitty shipwrecked on island in the South Seas

Circa 1840—Hitty sails from Bombay, India, to Philadelphia